This Walker book belongs to:

_____

_____

_____

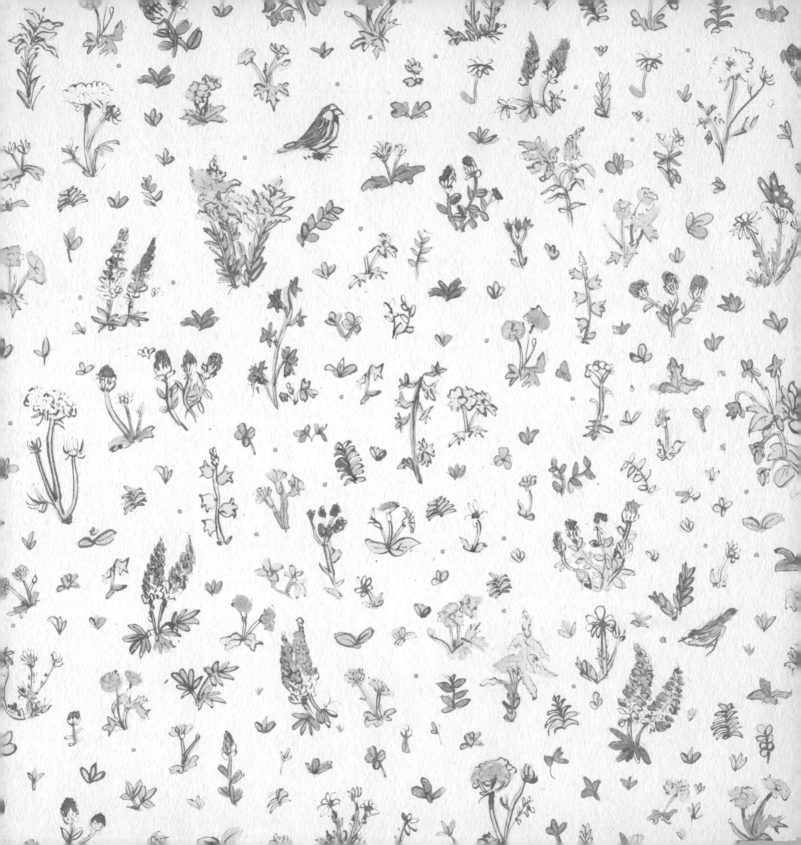

For Sophie, who showed me the
way, and for Amy, Ashey, and JoJo,
for being our destination. *JL*

For Sheila Barry and
Michael Solomon. Thank you for
believing in me. *SS*

Published in the UK in 2015 by Walker Books Ltd
87 Vauxhall Walk, London SE11 5HJ

This edition published 2016

First published in Canada and the USA as *Sidewalk Flowers* in 2015 by Groundwood Books

4 6 8 10 9 7 5

Text © 2015 JonArno Lawson
Illustrations © 2015 Sydney Smith

The right of JonArno Lawson and Sydney Smith to be identified as author and illustrator of this work
has been asserted by them in accordance with the Copyright, Designs and Patents Act 1988

The illustrations were done in ink and watercolour, with digital editing

Design by Michael Solomon

Printed in China

British Library Cataloguing in Publication Data:
catalogue record for this book is available from the British Library

ISBN 978-1-4063-6567-2

www.walker.co.uk

Footpath Flowers

JonArno Lawson   Sydney Smith

WALKER BOOKS
AND SUBSIDIARIES
LONDON • BOSTON • SYDNEY • AUCKLAND

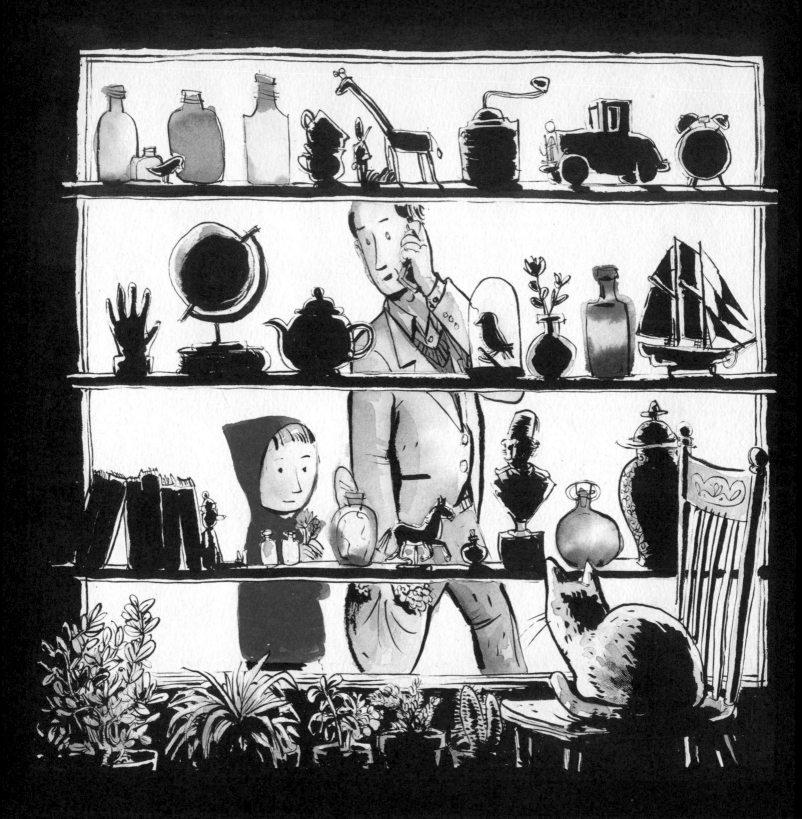

"I'd give this book to anyone with a coffee table" *New York Times*

"Cleverly and beautifully illustrated" *The School Librarian*

"A beautiful book with a powerful message" *Inis*

"A powerful reminder of the importance of appreciating our surroundings and the mutual gift of giving" *Junior* **magazine**

"A poignant, wordless storyline … this ode to everyday beauty sings sweetly" *Kirkus*, **starred review**

"An emotionally moving, visually delightful ode to the simple powers of observation and empathy… A book to savour slowly and then revisit again and again" *School Library Journal*, **starred review**

"A quiet, graceful book about the perspective-changing wonder of humble, everyday pleasures" *Booklist*, **starred review**

NOMINATED FOR THE KATE GREENAWAY MEDAL

**NOMINATED FOR THE GOODREADS CHOICE
AWARD FOR BEST PICTURE BOOK**